BEN M. BAGLIO

FROG FRIENDS

Illustrations by
Paul Howard

Cover Illustration by
Chris Chapman

A
LITTLE APPLE
PAPERBACK

SCHOLASTIC INC.

New York Toronto London Auckland Sydney
Mexico City New Delhi Hong Kong

ISBN 0-439-23025-X

12 11 10 9 8 7 6 5 4 3 2 1   2 3 4 5 6/0

Printed in the U.S.A.   40
First Scholastic printing, July 2001

FROG FRIENDS

Books in the Animal Ark Pets series

1 Puppy Puzzle
2 Kitten Crowd
3 Rabbit Race
4 Hamster Hotel
5 Mouse Magic
6 Chick Challenge
7 Pony Parade
8 Guinea Pig Gang
9 Gerbil Genius
10 Duckling Diary
11 Lamb Lessons
12 Doggy Dare
13 Cat Crazy
14 Ferret Fun
15 Bunny Bonanza
16 Frog Friends

Special thanks to Pat Posner

Contents

1. Pond Plans   1
2. Rescue Operation   20
3. Missing Frogs   38
4. Problems   55
5. Hatching Day   73
6. "Raining Frogs!"   90
7. Exciting News   99

FROG FRIENDS

1

Pond Plans

As Mandy Hope made her way to the village square, she wondered if James Hunter, her best friend, would already be waiting for her by the big oak tree. They always met there to walk to school together, but today she'd been a bit late leaving home.

When she drew close to the last of the stone

cottages behind the Fox and Goose pub, Mandy saw two orange cats sitting on top of a plastic-covered, barrel-shaped object. "Hello, Missie. Hello, Scraps," she said. "What *are* you sitting on?" she asked.

Mandy's parents were both vets, and their clinic, Animal Ark, was attached to the stone cottage where they lived. Mandy took great interest in Animal Ark's patients and knew most of the animals in Welford.

"Never you mind, young Mandy. You'll find out what it is soon enough." Mandy looked up to see old Walter Pickard standing in his cottage doorway, with his friend Ernie Bell.

"Hello, Mr. Pickard. Hello, Mr. Bell," said Mandy. "Is it something to do with the school garden?" she asked.

Over the last couple of months, parents, pupils, and friends of Welford Village Elementary School had been working on an old courtyard at the back of the school. They were going to leave the large wild patch as it was, but turn the rest into a garden with all sorts of different planting areas. Most of the digging and building work was finished and they'd already started sowing seeds and putting plants into the new flowerbeds.

Walter's eyes twinkled and he tapped the side of his nose with one large finger. "You'll just have to wait and see," he told her.

Mandy smiled. Then she heard the church clock striking in the distance. "I'd better go," she said. "James will be wondering where I am." Mandy stroked both the cats one last time and said good-bye to the two elderly men.

*   *   *

"Don't tell me," said James when Mandy came flying toward him. "You saw a cat or a dog and just had to stop to say hello."

"How did you guess?" Mandy laughed. Everyone knew she was animal-crazy. James loved animals nearly as much as Mandy did. He had an adorable Labrador puppy called Blackie and a cat called Benji.

"I stopped to stroke Missie and Scraps," Mandy explained. As they hurried along the main street, she told James how mysterious Walter had been when she'd asked what the cats were sitting on. "I can't think what it was," she said, "but I'm sure it must be something to do with the school garden."

"If it is, you'll find out soon enough," James said.

"Mmm. That's what Mr. Pickard said," replied Mandy.

"Well, then," grinned James, "you'll just have to be patient, won't you!"

Mandy groaned. She wasn't very good at waiting to find things out.

They arrived at the school playground just as the bell rang. Mandy was in fifth grade and James was in the year behind her, so they said good-bye and hurried off to join their own classes.

After homeroom, it was time to go to the school auditorium for assembly. At the end of assembly, Mrs. Garvie, the principal, stepped forward to make an announcement. "Thanks to the windy weather we've been having, the concrete base and sides of our new garden pond have set and dried much quicker than we expected," she said. "Later today, Mr. Pickard and Mr. Bell will be pumping water from the stream into the pond. And on Wednesday, Mr. Meakin from the garden center is coming to put in a selection of pond plants."

So that's *what was sitting outside Walter's,* thought Mandy as she joined the clapping and cheering. *A pump for pumping water!*

Mrs. Garvie held up a hand for silence, then she continued, "For the rest of this semester, all classes will be working on topics to do with the garden or pond. Your teachers will tell you about your projects later. I'm looking forward to seeing your work."

During their lunch break, James told Mandy that his class was making an instrument to measure rainfall. Later that afternoon Mrs. Todd told the fifth grade their topic was to be "Around Our School," which would involve making a map of the school grounds and garden.

"There's something else, too," Mrs. Todd continued. "Starting the week after next, for one lesson a week, some of you will be acting as helpers to the first- and second-graders when they're working in the school garden."

"That'll be great," said Mandy. She hoped she'd be chosen as a helper, as she loved getting to know the younger children.

Mandy was delighted to hear that she was to be Libby Masters's helper. Libby had a pet hen called Rhonda — her parents were chicken farmers.

"The younger classes will be finding out what wildlife is in the garden," said Mrs. Todd. "And they'll also be looking at the life cycle of frogs. This will probably mean a couple of trips to the pond in the village square to look at frogs' eggs."

Mandy beamed. She could remember when she'd learned about frogs. It would be fun doing it again. Just as the bell rang, Mandy had a terrific idea.

As they set off for home, Mandy told James what her class's garden topic was going to be. "And I've got a plan for making things more interesting for the younger ones. Well, for the whole school, really," she added. "I'm going to ask Mom and Dad if they can think of anything we can do to encourage the frogs to come and live in the school garden."

"That's a great idea," James said.

"And," Mandy continued, "we could go to Lilac Cottage after school tomorrow and ask

Grandpa if he's got any tips. He's got a special frog friend called Croaker that comes to his garden every year."

"Great!" James said. He always enjoyed visiting Mandy's grandparents. "I'd better tell Mom I'll be home late tomorrow," he said as they went their separate ways.

When Mandy arrived at Animal Ark, Dr. Adam was in the kitchen having a cup of tea before office hours began. "Hi, Dad!" said Mandy.

"I recognize that look on your face." Dr. Adam laughed. "You've got something to ask me!"

Mandy grinned and told him all about her school project. "It would be much more fun if we could study real, live frogs," she said eagerly. "Is there anything we can do to get them to come and live in the school garden?"

"Well," said her dad, "the pond's a good start. I'm sure Philip Meakin from the garden center will put in reeds, pondweeds, water lilies, and all sorts of other plants that will appeal to frogs. Maybe he could put a few large stones in the pond for the frogs to swim around or hop onto as well."

"Like an underwater playground?" asked Mandy.

"Something like that," Dr. Adam said, smiling.

"That's a good idea," said Mandy. "I'll ask Mrs. Todd about it tomorrow."

"And remember," Dr. Adam added, "frogs are amphibians. They spend a lot of time in the water, but they only actually *live* in it when they're young. So you'll need to think what sort of plants they'd like around their land home. If I were you I'd go and have a word with Grandpa about that."

Mandy smiled. "Just what I thought," she said. "James and I have already arranged to visit him after school tomorrow."

At school the next day, Mandy told Mrs. Todd about her idea.

During afternoon break, Mrs. Todd called

Mandy over. "Mrs. Garvie and the other teachers think your idea of trying to encourage frogs is an excellent one," she said. "And Mrs. Garvie is going to ask Mr. Meakin what he thinks about putting a few stones in the pond."

"That's great!" said Mandy. "Thank you, Mrs. Todd."

Mrs. Todd smiled. "There's just time before the end of break for you to tell your friends," she said.

Mandy gathered all her friends around her and told them about the plans for the school pond.

"So, now all we need are some good tips from Mandy's grandpa for the frogs' land home," said James when Mandy told him and the others the good news.

Mandy nodded happily. "I can't wait to talk to Grandpa!" she said.

An hour later, Mandy and James hurried up the path to Lilac Cottage. "Look, there's Grandpa — in his greenhouse," said Mandy.

Grandpa heard her voice and came out to

greet them. "Grandma's gone on a day trip with the Women's Club," he said, putting down his watering can. "So how are you both?"

"Oh, we're fine," said Mandy, grinning at James. "We've come to tell you the news about the school garden."

They took turns telling Grandpa all about the new pond. "And," Mandy ended, "we want to make the garden a place frogs will want to come to. Have you got any tips for us?"

"So *that's* the reason you came to see me," teased Grandpa, ruffling Mandy's hair.

"Mandy says you've got a frog that comes back here every year," said James.

"Croaker," said Grandpa, nodding. "I'm expecting him any day now."

"Has Croaker got a favorite spot?" James asked.

"He always comes to that patch over there, the one with all those big-leafed plants. It's a good place for him because it's shady. He probably feels safe when he's sitting under the leaves, hidden from view," said Grandpa.

"Maybe we should get some plants like that," suggested Mandy.

"I tell you what," said Grandpa. "Let's take a few cuttings from the plants that are growing there. I'll put them in some special soil for a few days to help them grow good, healthy roots. Then you can take them to school and plant them in the school garden."

"Can't we just dig up some of the plants, Grandpa?" Mandy asked.

Grandpa told her that the main plant in Croaker's patch, wintergreen, had very long stems that spread out underground. "It would be difficult to dig up, Mandy. Much better to take cuttings. It will only take a week or ten days for the roots to grow."

"We could work out the best places to put the wintergreen and start digging holes for it, while we're waiting for the roots to grow," said James.

"Would they grow quicker if we watered the soil first, Grandpa?" Mandy asked.

"They might, love," said Grandpa. "That's if

you two stop chattering long enough to let me take the cuttings!" he teased.

"If you don't need any help, Grandpa, we'd better be going," said Mandy. "I've got some reading homework to do. And on the way home I want to see if there are any frogs' eggs in the pond in the square."

"I've got to take Blackie for his afternoon walk," added James.

"Off you go then," Grandpa told them.

"Give Grandma my love," said Mandy. "And will you call me if you can think of any other ways to get frogs to live in the school garden?"

"I'll do that," said Grandpa. "See you both soon."

"I might have an idea," said James as he and Mandy walked to the village square.

"What is it, James?" said Mandy.

"I'll work on it later. If it's a success, I'll tell you about it tomorrow," James said mysteriously. "Come on," he added. "Race you to the pond."

Mandy sighed as she hurried after James. She knew he wouldn't tell her his idea before he was ready.

There weren't any frogs' eggs in the pond, but Mandy thought she saw a frog. "Just its back legs as it dived down to the bottom of the water," she said. "But I can't see it now."

"Well, we'd better be going," said James, moving off. "Blackie must be dying for his walk by now. See you tomorrow, Mandy."

"It worked, Mandy!" James said as they walked to school the next morning. "Look!" He opened his hand to show Mandy a white frog-like shape. "I made it out of modeling clay and left it to dry overnight," he said. "It needs painting in the right colors now. Then it'll look even more like a frog."

"It's very good, James," said Mandy. "But," she added, looking puzzled, "what has this frog got to do with getting *real* ones to come into the garden?"

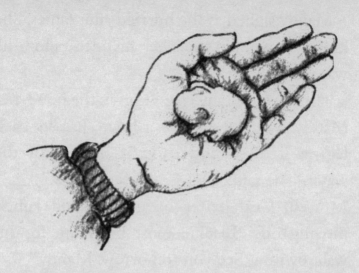

"Well, your dad said that frogs need a land home and, since they like leaping from one rock to another in the water, I thought it would be a good idea to have some near where we plant the wintergreen."

"And you thought of *making* rocks. Frog-shaped rocks!" said Mandy. "That's great, James."

James looked pleased. "I've got enough modeling clay to make lots more," he said. "I'm going to ask Mrs. Black if I can bring it to school. Then we could make the frogs during our breaks."

James's teacher liked his idea for frog-rocks. For the next few days James, Mandy, and their classmates spent most of their breaks making more clay frogs. Mrs. Black let the fourth grade paint them in their art lesson and soon there were dozens of "frog-rocks" in the flowerbeds and wild patch. One afternoon, Mrs. Black and Mrs. Todd stayed after school to help dig places for the wintergreen cuttings.

The next day at break Mandy kept glancing across to the pond. "Mr. Meakin has made the pond look like the perfect place for frogs," she said. "I just hope some frogs *will* find their way here, because if they do I'm sure they'll stay."

"And," said James, looking around at the frog-rocks, "when we've planted the wintergreen, the frogs will have great land playgrounds as well."

"We're going to Lilac Cottage after school tomorrow to see if the cuttings have grown roots," Mandy told their friends, crossing her fingers for good luck.

*   *   *

When Mandy and James arrived at Lilac Cottage, the next day, Grandpa told them that the cuttings had all grown good, healthy roots.

"That's great," said Mandy. She gave him a hug and grinned at her grandmother.

Just then, they heard the phone ringing from inside the cottage. "Come on in," said Grandma, hurrying up the path. "You put the kettle on while I answer the phone, Tom," she called over her shoulder to her husband.

"Grandma bought some rather nice ginger cookies when she went on her Women's Club trip last week," said Grandpa. "Let's have some of them with our drinks, and you can tell us what you've been doing at school this week."

"Blackie thinks that's an excellent idea," James laughed as they went into the kitchen. He and Mandy had brought Blackie from James's house before coming to Lilac Cottage.

By the time Grandma had finished on the phone, Grandpa had made the drinks and Mandy and James had put out some plates and opened the box of cookies. They'd just settled down around the kitchen table when Dr. Adam hurried in. "Hi, Dad," said Mandy, looking surprised.

"I tried to phone, but I couldn't get through," explained Dr. Adam. "We've got a problem. I've had a phone call from Farmer Jessop —"

"Is there something wrong with one of his cows?" Mandy asked anxiously. Farmer Jessop had recently begun dairy farming. Mandy loved his black Kerry cows with their upswept horns.

Dr. Adam shook his head. "This call is a rather unusual one," he said. "Dozens of frogs have fallen down the new cattle grid he's put in!"

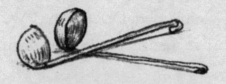

2

Rescue Operation

"I wanted to plant some chrysanthemums," said Grandpa, jumping up. "But I think rescuing frogs is more important."

"It's okay, Dad," Dr. Adam told his father. "Mr. Masters and young Libby were at the clinic fetching some special food for their new hens when Len phoned. They offered their help and have gone on ahead."

"There *is* something, though . . ." Dr. Adam added, looking at Grandma. "Could you spare any long-handled kitchen utensils please? Soup ladles, maybe?"

"Is *that* how we'll get the frogs out?" asked James. "With soup ladles?"

"I'm not sure until we get there," Dr. Adam replied. "But we might be able to use something like that to scoop the frogs up. I gave Mr. Masters two ladles and a bucket to take with him. I've also brought three buckets with lids that I've drilled airholes in."

"Come on, James. We'll get some canes and twine from my shed," Grandpa said. "You might need to make the ladles' handles longer, so they'll reach down to the frogs. And don't worry about your cuttings," he added. "I'll come and plant them for you tomorrow."

James put Blackie on his leash and hurried out after Grandpa.

"This takes me back to when your dad was young," Grandma said, passing Mandy two ladles and a spatula. "He used to go fishing for sticklebacks with my kitchen spoons!"

Mandy smiled and thanked her grandmother. "I'll call later to let you and Grandpa know how we manage," she said, then hurried after her dad to the Animal Ark Land Rover.

"How do you think the frogs got there, Dad?" Mandy asked as they drove along.

"I think they were probably trying to make their way to the pond on the far side of Lower Fell Farm," Dr. Adam said. "But the frogs falling into the cattle grid isn't the only problem."

"What do you mean, Dr. Adam?" asked James.

"Last time I was at the farm checking over one of the cows, I noticed that the pond had been filled in. Mr. Jessop said something had happened to the algae growing in the pond that caused a type of pollution and turned the water poisonous. Mr. Jessop felt filling it in was the safest thing to do, because children and animals often went near the pond."

"I'm glad it's been filled in then," Mandy said. "But what will we do with the frogs when we get them out, Dad?"

"We'll have to let them out near another pond or stream and just hope they produce their eggs there," he said.

"The school pond! Let's take them to the school pond!" Mandy and James yelled at the same time.

"I don't think Mrs. Garvie will mind," Mandy added. "She did say encouraging frogs was an excellent idea."

Dr. Adam laughed. "Your school pond will be as good a place as any," he agreed. "But don't count on them staying there to spawn."

Mandy was about to ask what her father meant, but by now they'd arrived at Lower Fell Farm. At first there was no sign of the farmer, or Mr. Masters and Libby. Mandy and James leaped out of the Land Rover, dashed to the cattle grid, and peered into it.

"Oh, the poor things!" Mandy gasped, staring at the dozens of frogs darting helplessly around at the bottom of the hollowed-out section, which was several feet below the grid's metal bars. "There's no water down there, and frogs die if their skin becomes too dry, don't they, Dad? We've got to get them out before that happens!"

"The ladles will easily go between the metal bars," said James. "But," he continued, lying flat on his stomach and demonstrating, "even though I can get most of my arm down, they're not long enough to reach anywhere near the bottom."

"Grandpa was right!" said Mandy, jumping to her feet. "We do need the canes and twine he gave us."

Just then, they heard a shout and looked up to see Farmer Jessop, Mr. Masters, and Libby coming down the field toward them. The men were carrying two buckets each, and Libby was struggling along with one smaller bucket.

"Great! They must be bringing water," said Mandy. "And look!" she added with a smile as she picked up a couple of canes and began ty-

ing them to the handle of a soup ladle, "Mr. Jessop's cows are following him!"

James joined her and started binding a cane to the handle of a ladle. "Water will help float the frogs nearer to the top, won't it?" he asked, looking toward Dr. Adam.

"It would take a lot of water to do that, James," Dr. Adam replied. "But once there's *some* water down there, the frogs will probably feel less panicky."

"We've brought a drink for the frogs," Libby called. "And we've also made your mom's soup spoons longer, Mandy," she added when she got close enough to see what Mandy and James were doing.

"Bring the ladles over here, Libby, and we'll see if they'll reach the bottom," said Mr. Masters when he and Farmer Jessop had carefully poured the water onto the frogs. "The frogs aren't moving around so much now," he added.

Mandy smiled when she heard some of the frogs croaking. "They're feeling better now that they've got some water," she said as she passed

James a lengthened ladle. Then she went over to the Land Rover to fetch the lidded buckets. Blackie whined pleadingly when Mandy opened up the back. "Okay, I guess you can come out," she said to him. "I'll tie your leash to the post at the side of the cattle grid and you can watch us rescue the frogs."

Dr. Adam told Mandy that he, Farmer Jessop, and Mr. Masters would reach down with the ladles and try to scoop the frogs into them. "Then we'll draw the ladles slowly upward. As soon as they're close enough to the top, you, James, and Libby can reach between the bars to pick up the frogs and pop them into the buckets," he explained.

But it wasn't as easy as Dr. Adam made it sound. It took some time to scoop the frogs onto the ladles. And when one of the men managed to get a ladle close to the top of the grid, the frogs jumped off before Mandy, James, or Libby could catch them. Mr. Masters decided to use a spatula. "I'll bend it at right angles, so it'll slide underneath the frog easily," he said. "That might be easier than trying to scoop one up with the ladle."

"It'll probably be easier to lift a frog off the spatula, too," added James.

Mr. Masters managed right away to get a frog on the spatula — and to get it close to the top of the grid.

James got hold of the frog . . . but then it shot out of his hand as he pulled it up from between two bars. "Don't you know we're trying to help you?" he asked.

A frog leaped out of Libby's hand and plopped back down to the bottom of the cattle grid. She shrieked in disappointment.

"I think you're too worried about hurting the frogs when you pick them up," Dr. Adam told them. "Hold them a bit more firmly."

"You're right, Dr. Adam!" James said a couple of seconds later. "I've got one. Quick, Mandy, take the lid off one of the buckets. This frog is definitely going in it."

"Great!" said Mandy, popping the lid back on the bucket the second James took his hand away.

Mandy was the next to catch a frog, then James quickly got another two. Blackie was fascinated by all the activity. He wriggled his way closer and closer to the edge of the grid.

"You've brought me luck, Blackie," said Libby when she finally managed to pick a frog off her dad's spatula and get it all the way to the bucket without it jumping out of her hand.

It was a very slow process, but at last there was only one frog left beneath the cattle grid. "It's a really dark green," said Mandy, looking down at it. "I'm sure it's much darker than the others."

"It looks like the clay frog Amy Fenton painted," James said. "She didn't let the green paint dry properly before she painted on the black markings. And it ended up a blacky-green color. *No,* Blackie! I wasn't saying your name," he added, laughing as his dog whined and wagged his tail.

Just then, Mr. Jessop got to his feet and glanced anxiously at his cows. They'd been crowded together in the field, calmly watching what was going on. But now they were beginning to get restless.

"You'd better let us do the rest, Len," said Dr. Adam, standing up and following Farmer Jessop's gaze. "It must be milking time for your ladies."

"Yes, we'll soon have the last frog safely with his friends," Mandy said, smiling up at the farmer. "It's such a good thing you saw them, Mr. Jessop."

"I've been keeping a regular check, Mandy,"

Mr. Jessop told her. "The frogs have crossed my fields to get to their pond for as long as I can remember. They're later than usual this year, though. I expect that's because March was so cold."

"It's lucky the frogs were late," Mandy said thoughtfully. "Our school pond wouldn't have been finished if they'd come earlier."

"So that's where you're taking them," said Mr. Jessop. Then, as one of his cows gave a long, drawn-out moo, the farmer stepped quickly over the grid and hurried toward them. "Good luck!" he called as he tapped one of the cows lightly on her behind to turn her around.

The cow turned and so did the rest of the herd. The sudden noise of them all moving together frightened Blackie. The puppy panicked, moving forward onto the cattle grid. Suddenly, his front legs slipped down between the metal bars.

"Blackie!" James cried as his dog let out a howl.

Dr. Adam spun around to bend over the

frightened dog. "It's all right, James. He isn't hurt. He just gave himself a fright, that's all. Come on, fellow, up you go." Dr. Adam lifted the dog and put him gently down on the grass, away from the grid.

Mandy knelt down beside Blackie, stroking and soothing him. While she was busy doing that, Mr. Masters finally managed to scoop the dark-green frog up from the grid and put it in one of the buckets.

Blackie had quickly got over his fright and was rolling on his back to have his tummy tickled. "He's a big faker!" James said as Libby knelt down beside the puppy and held one of his waving paws. "You only howled like that to get a bit of attention, didn't you? Well, you've had enough now. We've got to get these frogs over to the school pond."

"I didn't realize there'd be so many frogs," said Mandy, looking worried. "Do you think we should phone Mrs. Garvie and make sure it will be okay to take them there, Dad?"

"I'll phone her from my car phone, while

you bring the buckets," said Dr. Adam, moving toward the Land Rover.

Mandy nodded and helped Libby carry the bucket she'd picked up. "Won't it be fun if they lay their eggs in our pond?" she said as they walked toward the car. "You'll love watching the baby tadpoles wriggling around when they hatch out of their jelly, Libby."

Libby slowed down. Frowning, she looked up at Mandy.

"The little black specks inside frog spawn are frogs' eggs," Mandy explained. "Frogs' eggs hatch into tadpoles and tadpoles turn into baby frogs."

"I know that, Mandy!" said Libby. "I just don't want to hear about babies right now."

Mandy wondered why, but just then Dr. Adam popped his head out of the Land Rover window and gave a thumbs-up sign. "Mrs. Garvie says it's okay," he said.

"*Yes!*" shouted Mandy and James. They hurried to put the buckets in the back of the Land Rover.

Mr. Masters put his bucket in. He said he and Libby had better get home to take care of the hens.

"We'll see you at school tomorrow, Libby," said James as he, Blackie, and Mandy climbed into the car.

"And so will the frogs!" Mandy called through the open window as Dr. Adam moved across to the driving seat and put on his seat belt.

"How should we release them, Dad?" Mandy asked as they walked across the school playground toward the garden and pond. "Do we just tip the frogs into the pond from the buckets?"

Dr. Adam shook his head, "I think it will be best if they find the water for themselves," he said. "We'll lay the buckets down on the grassy area close to the edge of the pond, take off the lids, and wait to see what happens."

Mandy and James knelt down beside the buckets and removed the lids. They waited eagerly for the frogs to make their way out.

"The silly things want to stay in the buckets!" James whispered after a couple of minutes.

"Tip the buckets slightly," Dr. Adam suggested quietly. "Like this," he added, gently lifting the base of the bucket to tilt it.

Sure enough, the frogs slowly started to come out of all three buckets. Some sank themselves down into the grass, but a few began to hop and leap around. "Look," Mandy said quietly, "there's that dark-green one. We ought to give it a name, James."

"Let's call it Legs," James suggested, "because it's got especially long black legs."

Mandy smiled. Then she pointed. "Legs has gone really close to the pond. If only she'd jump in, I'm sure the others would hear the plop and follow," she said. And, almost as soon as Mandy had stopped speaking, they heard a small splashing sound. Then another, and another.

"At least three have gone into the water," said James, "but I didn't see any of them doing it."

They waited a while longer and, suddenly,

they saw one frog after another leaping into the pond. "Can we go closer, Dad?" Mandy asked hopefully.

"Best to leave that until morning," Dr. Adam replied. "The frogs have had quite an unsettling time with everything that's happened to them."

Mandy gave a small sigh. She was longing to see if the frogs were swimming around the rocks that Mr. Meakin had put in the pond, or find out if they were having swimming races from one end to the other. But she knew she'd have to do as her dad said and wait until the morning.

3

Missing Frogs

"I can't see a single frog, can you, James?" Mandy asked.

Dr. Emily had given them a lift to school so they'd arrive nice and early. Now they were kneeling at the edge of the pond, using sticks to gently push aside the reeds and to lift the leaves of the big water lily plants. The water lilies weren't floating yet; the leaves were below the surface of the water. Mr. Meakin had told them it would be another month before the plants would float or get their flowers.

James sighed and shook his head. "But they might be hiding on the bottom of the pond," he said. "Or under the rocks," he added.

"Maybe they can see us even though we can't see them," Mandy whispered. "Let's move back a bit."

"Okay," agreed James.

They stood quietly for a few minutes, but the only thing they saw was a whirligig beetle dancing on the surface of the water. Then the bell rang and they had to dash to the playground and line up with their classes.

After assembly, Mandy told her classmates all about the rescue operation and bringing the frogs to the school garden. "But this morning James and I looked and we couldn't see any!" she added sadly.

"Could we search for the missing frogs during our breaks, Mrs. Todd?" Peter Foster asked. "They might have hopped out of the pond and gone into some other part of the garden."

Mrs. Todd agreed. "But now it's time for the first lesson, so get out your books and let's begin."

Mandy tried to concentrate but she couldn't stop herself from looking at the clock every few minutes. At last it was time for a break and everyone hurried outside. "Mrs. Todd said we could look for the frogs," she told James as soon as she saw him.

"I asked Mrs. Black, too," James said.

They split into little groups to search in different parts of the garden. Mandy, James, and Lisa Glover looked in the clumps of daffodils in the wild patch. There were lots of daffodils. Every year, when the classroom bulbs finished flowering, they were taken out of their pots and planted in the wild patch.

When Lisa Glover called out in excitement, Mandy and James ran over to her. "Sorry," she said, turning red. "I thought I saw a frog, but then I realized it was one of the clay ones!"

Nobody saw any real frogs. They looked again during lunch. Grandpa Hope arrived to plant the wintergreen cuttings. He saw Mandy, who was peering into a holly bush.

"Have you spotted a bird's nest, Mandy?" he asked.

Mandy shook her head and explained about the missing frogs. "Well, I'll keep a lookout while I'm doing my planting," he said. "If I see any, I'll slip into the school and ask the school secretary to let you know."

"Thanks, Grandpa," said Mandy. "I'll be able to work better this afternoon, now that I know someone's still looking."

"I've been keeping an eye open for Croaker in my garden," said Grandpa. "I'm getting quite worried about him. He's usually here by now."

"Maybe he was one of the frogs we rescued," said Mandy. "He might be making his way to Lilac Cottage right now, Grandpa."

Mandy felt quite gloomy when she and James left school to go home. "We've looked for

41

the frogs on and off all day," she said. "And Grandpa can't have seen any or he'd have sent a message to us."

James nodded. After that, they walked along without talking very much.

But as they slowed down near the crossroads, James looked at Mandy and said thoughtfully, "Why did your dad say we shouldn't be disappointed if the frogs didn't stay in our pond?"

Mandy said she'd just been thinking about that as well. "I'll ask him as soon as I get home," she said. "Then I'll call and tell you," she added, before running off.

When she reached Animal Ark, Mandy burst in through the clinic door.

"What's the hurry, Mandy?" Jean Knox, the receptionist, asked.

"I need to talk to Dad before office hours begin. Is he here, Jean?"

Jean nodded. "He's with your mom in the unit, giving the animals their medicine."

"Thanks, Jean." Mandy rushed toward the

unit. This was where animals stayed if they were too sick to go home, or if they'd been kept in for observation. She slowed down before pushing open the unit door. She knew a sudden noise could upset the animals.

There were two cats, a guinea pig, and a rabbit in the unit but, for once, Mandy didn't stop in front of each animal's cage to say a few words.

Dr. Adam appeared from behind another row of cages and Mandy hurried over to him. "The frogs are gone, Dad," she said. "They weren't in the pond when James and I looked first thing, so we searched all over the garden. Why did you think they might not stay, Dad?"

"Well," he said, "frogs usually go back to the same breeding site, year after year. I read somewhere that even frogs that aren't old enough to lay eggs go back to the pond they were born in."

"So do you think some of them have made their way to where Farmer Jessop's pond used to be?" Mandy asked, feeling worried. "And, if they have, what will they do when they find it isn't there anymore?"

"Some of them might go off and find another pond — one of their own choice," Dr. Adam explained. "But if there are puddles and damp areas near where the pond was, I think it's more likely that the frogs would lay their eggs there."

"But what happens if there isn't enough water?" asked Mandy.

"Well," Dr. Adam replied, "even if the eggs stay alive, which is doubtful, there certainly wouldn't be enough water for the tadpoles once they've eaten their way out of the jelly."

"Can James and I go and see if the frogs are at the filled-in pond?" Mandy asked. "If they've laid their eggs in puddles, we could take them to the school pond."

"First a frog rescue, then a frogs'-egg rescue!" said Dr. Emily as she walked toward them pushing the medicine cart.

"Does that mean I can go?" said Mandy. "Thanks, Mom."

Dr. Emily handed her a package of rubber gloves from the cart. "You and James should wear gloves if you find any frogs' eggs to collect. And tell James not to take Blackie. You don't want to risk him drinking any water that might still be polluted. There are some empty jars in the cupboard under the kitchen sink," she added.

"I'll call Mr. Jessop and tell him you're going up there," Dr. Adam said.

Mandy grinned at her parents and hurried off to phone James and get the jars.

As Mandy and James started to make their way through the field toward the filled-in pond, James suddenly stopped and then turned in a slow circle. "What *are* you doing?" Mandy asked, looking puzzled.

James turned back to face her with a triumphant grin. "I was working out the route from the school garden to this field. I was checking that if the frogs have come here, they wouldn't have had to cross the cattle grid again."

"Gosh, I never even thought of that!" Mandy said. "It would have been awful if we'd had to scoop them all out *again*!"

They continued walking. Suddenly they heard a strange *grook-grook-grook*ing noise. Mandy gave an excited squeak and grabbed James's arm. "I

46

think it's the frogs," she said. "It is, James! Look!"

There were about forty or fifty frogs sitting in huddled groups in puddles and damp patches. Their eyes looked enormous and, as Mandy and James crept closer, they noticed that the pouched area under every frog's throat was puffed out. Mandy thought it looked as if each frog was blowing up a balloon. She put her hand over her mouth to stop herself from giggling out loud.

"That noise must be coming from their throats," said James. "I can't see any of them opening their mouths."

"Maybe they can make a louder noise when they do it that way," said Mandy. "I bet all the frogs for miles around can hear them."

"They must be saying 'come and join us,'" James said. "Let's split up and creep around to see if there's any frogs' eggs anywhere."

Although it hadn't rained for a while, there were quite a few puddles and wet, boggy places where the pond had once been. "There are lots of twigs over there," said Mandy, pointing toward a hedge. "Let's get some to mark every puddle and boggy patch. That way, we won't keep looking in the same place twice."

They both got very muddy feet walking around the puddles, and every time they stuck a twig into a boggy patch they got mud on their hands as well. By the time Mandy remembered she had rubber gloves with her, their hands were too dirty to put them on. Neither of them saw any eggs. "But we can come back over the weekend to check," said James.

"Next time we'll wear gloves," said Mandy, wiping her hands on some grass.

"And boots," added James, looking down at his filthy shoes and legs.

When the friends returned early the next morning, the frogs were still croaking — but not as noisily — and Mandy's eyes lit up as she saw some clumps of eggs floating on top of the deepest puddles. She handed James a pair of rubber gloves and they walked from puddle to puddle, scooping the jellylike masses into their containers.

"I wonder how many eggs each frog lays?" said James. "There must be hundreds in this clump, Mandy. It's taking ages to get it into the jar."

"Push with the jar *and* with your hand," suggested Mandy. "Like this, James. Watch."

"You're the expert!" James laughed as Mandy's clump of frogs' eggs slid right over her jar and back into the puddle.

"It worked the other times," said Mandy. But she was laughing, too.

Ten minutes later, they'd got all the eggs into their containers. "School pond, here we come!" James announced.

"And we'll come back after lunch to see if you've laid any more eggs," Mandy told the frogs as they walked past a small group of them.

There weren't any more frogs' eggs that evening, but on Sunday morning there were a lot more. And there were some more in the af-

ternoon, as well. Dr. Adam, on his way back from a call, saw Mandy and James and stopped to give them a lift.

"Come and help us put it in the pond, Dad," Mandy said when they arrived outside the school.

Dr. Adam congratulated them on how much frog spawn they'd rescued. "But," he said with a smile, "I think you should make this the last batch. You don't want to overcrowd the pond. The tadpoles won't develop well if there are too many of them. Besides, the frogs will probably have finished laying eggs now," he added, seeing Mandy's worried look.

"And I suppose it's best to let *these* tadpoles grow into healthy, lively frogs," said Mandy.

"That's my girl!" said Dr. Adam.

Next day, Mandy and James told their friends and teachers about the frogs' eggs they'd brought to the school pond. "I was so disappointed when the frogs didn't stay," Mandy explained to Mrs. Todd. "But I'm happy about that now. It will be really useful to have our own frogs' eggs, so the younger ones can look at them while they're learning about frogs."

Mrs. Todd laughed. "Something tells me *all* of you will take this opportunity to relearn the life cycle of frogs," she said. "However, you won't be working with the first and second grades until the end of the week. So, until then, apart from breaks, I want you to start concentrating on our own report. This morning, we're going outside to measure distances. I want you to write down the different places you think we should show on our map of the school grounds and garden."

But once the fifth-graders got outside, Mrs. Todd led them over to the pond so everyone could see the frogs' eggs.

"I think Mrs. Todd is just as interested in our frogs-to-be as we are," Mandy said to Jill Redfern, her eyes shining.

By Thursday, when Mandy paired up with Libby for a lesson, the black specks in the frog spawn had grown larger inside the masses of jelly.

"I wonder which tadpoles will be the first to come out," said Mandy, glancing around the pond. "Those look bigger than the others, don't they, Libby?" she said, pointing toward a patch of spawn underneath a plant with pink flowers.

"I think the tadpoles in the jelly by the reeds

will hatch first," said Susan Davis, one of Libby's classmates. "Let's bet on it."

There was no response from Libby. When Mandy turned her head to glance at her, the younger girl had turned her back to the pond and was staring across toward the wild patch. "Libby, don't you want to guess which tadpoles will hatch first?" Mandy asked.

Libby shrugged, then she said, "Let's go and look for ladybugs in the wild patch, Mandy."

Libby didn't talk much while she and Mandy searched. Mandy wondered if Libby and Susan had had a fight. "Aren't you and Susan getting along?" Mandy asked at last.

"Yes," said Libby. "It's just that she thinks baby tadpoles are interesting. I think they're boring."

Mandy got the distinct impression that Libby didn't want to talk about it anymore.

4

Problems

When Mandy got home from school she found her mom in the kitchen of Animal Ark, making a cup of tea.

"Have you had a good day, love?" Dr. Emily asked as she gave Mandy a quick hug.

"Yes, fine," Mandy said. Then she sighed and said worriedly, "I was helping Libby with her class report today, Mom. She didn't even *look* at the frogs' eggs. Then we went into the wild patch to look for ladybugs because she said that was what she wanted to do. But even then she was really quiet."

"That doesn't sound like Libby," Dr. Emily agreed.

"I wondered if she was worrying about the new hens," said Mandy. "Have you heard how they are, Mom?"

"Mrs. Masters phoned to say most of them have picked up really well," Dr. Emily said. "There's just one, now, who needs extra attention. But you'll be able to see for yourself on Sunday — Mrs. Masters has invited you and James to lunch. And Grandma called. You haven't been to see her for a while, you know. Why don't you go around after school tomorrow? I've got a couple of afternoon farm visits, so I could pick you up on my way back."

"Okay," said Mandy. "I'll call James and see if he wants to come, too."

*   *   *

"It's such a lovely day, I thought we'd have our snack in the garden," Grandma suggested when Mandy, James, and Blackie arrived at Lilac Cottage the next day. "I've put a few dog biscuits in a bowl for you, Blackie," she added, bending to stroke the puppy.

"It is a nice day, isn't it?" said Mandy after hugging her grandma and grandpa. "I'm glad it's warm — it might help the tadpoles to hatch quicker. They're getting quite big now, aren't they, James?"

"Yup," James said, but he was looking longingly at the picnic table.

"Let Blackie off the leash and give him his bowl of biscuits, James," said Grandma. She moved to the table, removed the white cloth covering the food, and passed James a plastic bowl.

"Thanks, Mrs. Hope," said James. "These are his favorite."

"Blackie likes *any* sort of food." Mandy laughed as she sat down next to Grandpa. Blackie had gobbled down the biscuits almost before James had sat down in the chair next to Grandma.

The puppy bounded over to the table and looked pleadingly up at James. "Go away, Blackie," said James. "You've had yours."

To everyone's surprise, Blackie turned around and made his way down to the bottom of the garden. "He must have decided to get a drink from the trough instead, seeing as he can't get any more food," Mandy said.

But, instead of getting a drink, Blackie began sniffling and snuffling in the long grass growing around the bottom of the trough.

"I think he's found something!" James said, suddenly jumping to his feet and racing off toward his pet.

"What is it?" asked Grandpa as he, Grandma, and Mandy all jumped up to follow James.

By the time they reached the end of the garden, James had a firm hold on Blackie's collar. The Labrador glanced sadly at his master, then strained his head forward again to stare into the grass.

Grandpa dropped on to his knees and parted the long grass. "It's a frog," he said quietly. "And," he added, gazing down, "I'm almost sure it's Croaker."

"He's certainly about the same size as him," Grandma agreed, peering over Grandpa's shoulder. "Thank heavens for that," she whispered to Mandy. "Grandpa's been wondering for days if Croaker was coming back this year."

"The little fellow doesn't look quite right," Grandpa said, shaking his head. "He looks as if there's a heavy weight pressing him down into the grass."

Mandy knelt down beside Grandpa. "Maybe he's just trying to hide himself from us," she suggested.

"I'm almost sure Blackie didn't *touch* him," James said, looking worried.

"I don't think he's injured," Grandpa said, peering closely at the frog. "I can't see any marks on him. But there's something wrong, I'm sure there is. His sides look a bit swollen to me."

"Mom's coming to get me and James," said Mandy. "She can tell us if there's something wrong with Croaker."

"Go and get me a bucket, Mandy, love," Grandpa said. "We'll put some damp grass in it and make him a nest."

Mandy raced off. James put Blackie on his leash and tied him to the fence. Then he helped Grandma pick some long grass and dampen it in the trough.

When Mandy came back, she'd brought a tea towel as well. "We can cover the bucket with it, just in case he tries to hop out," she said.

"Good girl," Grandpa said. "I don't think he will try to hop out," he added as he pressed the damp grass into a nest shape. "But the towel will make it nice and dark inside the bucket. It's often best to put sick creatures in a quiet, dark place."

Carefully he picked Croaker up and put him into the bucket. "His skin feels really rough. I'm sure it should be cold and damp," said

Grandpa. "Maybe he's not been drinking enough water."

"I'm sure Mom will know how to make him better," said Mandy as she covered the bucket with the tea towel.

Dr. Emily arrived a few minutes later and Mandy dashed to the gate. She was explaining about the frog almost before her mom had had time to get out of the car.

"I'm glad you're here, Emily," said Grandpa as Mandy and Dr. Emily came into the garden. He removed the tea towel from the bucket and Mandy's mom picked Croaker up. She ran her fingers all over his body.

"If this *is* Croaker," she said, glancing up at Grandpa, "he's a *she*. That's why her skin feels dry. At egg-laying time, female frogs develop a rough skin to let the male frogs know they're looking for a mate."

"And," Dr. Emily added, "Croaker is egg-bound."

"What does that mean, Dr. Emily?" asked James.

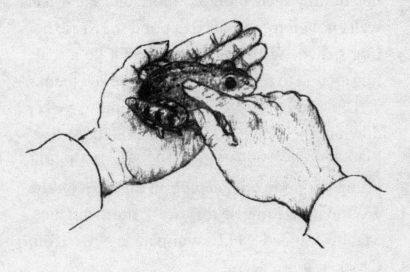

"For some reason, Croaker can't release her eggs — the frog spawn," Dr. Emily explained. "I think the poor creature has got a rather nasty tummyache." She put Croaker back into the nest of damp grass and, using her forefingers, stroked the frog's sides, pressing gently.

"Are you trying to move the eggs that are inside her?" Mandy asked.

Dr. Emily nodded. "Rubbing her like this should help," she said. "Then, hopefully, when her tummy feels more comfortable, she'll feel well enough to hop off to a pond to release her frog spawn. With any luck, there'll be a male frog around to fertilize the eggs as she lays them."

A few minutes later, Dr. Emily put Croaker down in the long grass near the trough. At first, the frog stayed still. Then she rose up slightly, lifting her body but keeping all four legs on the ground. She jumped forward a short distance. Mandy smiled and whispered, "Go on, Croaker. Jump again."

Croaker did jump again. And again and again. Before long, she hopped under the hedge and disappeared from view.

"Looks like that tummy-rubbing cured the little fellow," said Grandpa.

"Grandpa!" Mandy laughed.

"What? Oh, yes," Grandpa chuckled. "Croaker isn't a he . . . she's a she. And I hope *she* comes back to her patch when she's laid her frog spawn. Now, James, go and untie Blackie. He must be feeling neglected after all that."

"We'll have to be going anyway," said Dr. Emily. "I have my yoga class tonight."

As Grandma and Grandpa waved good-bye, Grandpa called, "Keep a lookout for Croaker. If you see him hopping down the road, get out and move him to a safe place."

"It will take Grandpa ages to remember Croaker's a female frog!" Mandy giggled. "I bet Libby will like hearing all about it when we go there for lunch," she added.

"You can tell her about Stella's puppies, too," said Dr. Emily. "She had them this morning. Two boys and two girls."

Stella was the Jessops' Australian cattle dog. "What color are the puppies, Mom?" Mandy asked. "Have they got blue patches like Stella?" Mandy had only seen Stella once, but she remembered the dog looked a bit like a German shepherd. Her coat had shades of blue mixed in with her black and tan markings.

"The puppies are born white," Dr. Emily replied.

"Oh, I bet they look gorgeous!" Mandy said. "How long do they stay white? Do you think Mrs. Jessop will let James and me see them before their color changes?"

Dr. Emily said that the puppies' color would start developing gradually when they were around three weeks old. "I told Mrs. Jessop I'd call on Sunday to make sure Stella's coping all right," said Dr. Emily. "So, we could go together, after I've picked you up from Libby's, and you can look at the puppies then."

"That'll be great," said James. "*And* we can let Farmer Jessop know what stage the frog spawn has reached."

On Sunday, when James and Mandy arrived at Blackheath Farm, Mandy was really surprised to see that Libby's mom was expecting a baby.

Mrs. Masters smiled when she noticed Mandy's surprise. "I was probably bundled up in my warm jacket the last time you saw me," she explained. "That's why you didn't notice."

Mandy nodded, but she was wondering why Libby hadn't said anything. Wasn't Libby excited about having a new brother or sister?

"Aren't you going to say hello to your visitors, Libby?" asked Mrs. Masters. Libby was paying careful attention to setting the table.

"Hello, James. Hello, Mandy," said Libby.

"Hi, Libby. You look very busy," said Mandy.

"Mom let me make a big red and orange Jell-O mold for dessert," said Libby. "I made it with peach juice and peaches."

"That sounds delicious," said James. "I can't wait to try it!"

"Do you want to help me put all the food on the table?" said Libby. "Then we can have lunch right away. When we've finished, we can go and see Rhonda and the new hens."

"I'll go outside to find Dad and tell him lunch won't be long," Mrs. Masters said to Libby.

"All right," she said without looking at her mom.

Mandy felt puzzled as she walked to the countertop to get a plate of sandwiches. Libby had sounded quite strange, almost unfriendly, when she'd answered her mother.

There was a short silence, then James said, "You'll never guess what Blackie found on Friday, Libby."

"Tell me, James," said Libby. "I love hearing about Blackie."

That's more like Libby, Mandy thought thankfully as she took a bowl of salad to the table.

James started to tell Libby about Blackie and Croaker, and Libby seemed really interested. ". . . Then Dr. Emily told us Croaker was a female frog who needed her tummy rubbed so she could go and lay her frog spawn!" James continued.

"I'll go and see if Mom and Dad are coming," Libby interrupted. "You two sit down. Everything's on the table now."

James looked at Mandy and shrugged. "You're right," he said, "Libby does seem different from usual. I think there's something wrong."

When Libby came back in with her mom and dad, Mr. Masters was carrying a basket of eggs. "There are six for each of you to take home when you go," he said to Mandy and James.

"That's great, Mr. Masters. Thank you," said James.

Mandy smiled at Libby's dad as he came and sat next to her. "I love having farm-fresh eggs for breakfast," she said. "*And* for lunch," she added as Mrs. Masters offered her the bowl of salad and hard-boiled eggs.

"Do you know which hen laid these eggs, Libby?" James asked.

Libby shook her head. "I didn't collect them this morning," she said. "I made the Jell-O instead."

After that, Libby hardly spoke. She barely looked up from the table at all. Even when James had a second helping of Jell-O and said,

"It tastes as good as it looks, Libby," she just gave him a tight little smile.

But when Mr. Masters said it was time to round up the hens, Libby jumped up happily enough. "Come on!" she said to Mandy and James.

"Okay," said Mandy. Then she looked at the basket of eggs Mr. Masters had brought in. "Can we put the eggs in cartons first, Mrs. Masters?" she asked. "That way, we'll be all ready to go when Mom comes to get us."

"Come and find me when you've done it, then," said Libby, and she hurried out after her dad.

Mrs. Masters sighed. "I'm afraid Libby isn't very happy about the new baby," she said as she passed Mandy two egg cartons. "At the moment, she doesn't like us to talk about babies at all. Not even baby animals."

"So *that's* why she said baby tadpoles are boring," said Mandy.

"And why she didn't want to hear about Croaker," added James.

As Mandy closed the egg-carton lids, she said, "I bet Libby will cheer up as soon as she sees her little brother or sister."

"I hope she cheers up before that," Mrs. Masters said, sounding worried. "I think Libby's jealous at the *thought* of sharing us with a new baby when he or she arrives." Then she added, "The baby isn't due until the middle of July. I'd hate to think of Libby being this unhappy for another three months!"

"We'll have to think of a way to cheer Libby

up!" Mandy said as she and James made their way outside.

James nodded. Then the two friends fell silent as they both tried to think of a way to help Libby.

5

Hatching Day

"Libby seems okay at the moment," James said in a low voice.

Mandy followed her friend's gaze. She smiled when she saw Libby skipping toward them with a large Rhode Island Red hen dancing along beside her.

"Rhonda was just coming to find you,"

laughed Libby. "She was fed up with waiting."

Mandy crouched down, making crooning noises. Rhonda the hen moved faster and, when she reached Mandy, she hopped up onto her lap. Mandy stroked her red feathers and Rhonda's head moved slowly up and down in contentment.

"Me now, Rhonda," James said, bending down next to Mandy and tapping his knees. He beamed with delight as Rhonda stepped from Mandy's lap onto his.

After a few more minutes of fussing over Rhonda, Libby said, "Come on, I'll show you the new hens."

Mr. Masters was filling the hens' food container when they went into the enclosure in front of the hen house. "That special diet food your mom recommended has really improved the hens' condition, Mandy," he said.

"Even Heather's getting better," said Libby, pointing to one of the smallest hens. "She's got a throat problem. We've been giving her cod-liver oil and lots of greens to eat. The rest of the new hens aren't very tame yet," Libby added. "But Heather will eat out of your hand. Can James and Mandy give her some food, Dad?"

Mr. Masters smiled, then he reached into the large pocket in his overalls and pulled out a brown paper bag. "Sprout leaves," he explained, giving Mandy and James a small handful each.

"Here, Heather. *Chuck-chuck-chuck,*" said James, holding out some leaves. Heather immediately left the other hens and walked toward him.

"She's really gentle, isn't she?" said Mandy, watching as the little hen took the leaves from James's fingers.

"Let's go back and see Rhonda again now," suggested Libby.

"Can Heather come with us?" Mandy asked.

"I don't think Rhonda likes Heather," Libby said sadly. "I've been trying to get them to make friends, but Rhonda won't."

They played with Rhonda until Mandy's

mom arrived. While Dr. Emily was petting the hen, Mrs. Masters came out with their eggs and Mandy and James thanked her for having them.

"You must come again soon," said Mrs. Masters. "Libby and Rhonda love having visitors."

"Yes, we do," Libby agreed. "We'll walk to the Land Rover with you to say good-bye, won't we, Rhonda?"

"We're stopping in at Lower Fell Farm on the way back, Libby," Dr. Emily said as they walked across to where she'd parked. "I suppose Mandy told you about Stella's white puppies. They're the most adorable babies!"

Oh, no! Mandy thought. *Why did Mom have to go and mention baby animals?*

Libby scowled, then looked down at Rhonda. "Come on, Rhonda. Time to go back," she said. And she turned around and walked off without even saying good-bye.

Mandy sighed as they got into the Land Rover. Once they'd set off, she told her mom what Mrs. Masters had told her.

"Poor Libby," said Dr. Emily. "But she probably just needs more time to get used to the idea of a new baby."

"I hope you're right, Mom," said Mandy. She knew it wasn't her mom's fault for mentioning Stella's puppies, but it felt like all the fun they'd had with Heather and Rhonda had been spoiled.

Mandy cheered up when they arrived at

Lower Fell Farm. Mrs. Jessop was sweeping the yard, and she hurried over to greet them. "I suppose you'd like to come and see the new arrivals?" she said to Mandy and James.

"Yes, please!" they said, scrambling out of the Land Rover.

"There are no problems at all," Mrs. Jessop said to Dr. Emily as she led the way into the kitchen. "Stella's a really good mom and the puppies are all feeding well."

Stella jumped out of the large box that was in one corner of the room and came toward them wagging her tail. Dr. Emily checked her over and said that she was fine.

Mandy and James petted Stella for a while, but then she moved away and started to make her way back to her puppies. When she was halfway to the box she turned and gave a small whine.

"Is she asking us to follow her, do you think?" asked Mandy.

"Looks like it," Mrs. Jessop replied with a smile.

Stella seemed really proud of her four white puppies, who were wriggling around in a heap at one end of the box. She wagged her tail harder and harder when Mandy and James knelt down by the box to get a closer look at them. They didn't pick up the puppies but gently stroked the tops of their heads.

"They're all lovely, Stella," said Mandy. "I think this one's my favorite, though," she said, smiling up at Mrs. Jessop. "She's got a really cute nose!"

Mrs. Jessop smiled. "She's going to be the mailman's puppy," she said. "The minute Bill Ward saw the puppies, yesterday morning, he decided he and his wife would like one. He picked out that female, there and then. He's calling her Tara."

"She'll grow up with Delilah," James said. "That's great." Delilah was Bill Ward's Persian kitten. Her mother, Duchess, belonged to Richard Tanner — one of Mandy and James's school friends.

After a while, Stella climbed back into the box, and sniffed and licked each puppy in turn. "She's settling down to feed them now," said Dr. Emily. "Come on, you two. Time to go."

Mandy and James thanked Mrs. Jessop for letting them see the puppies and followed Dr. Emily outside.

Just before they set off, Farmer Jessop hurried up and asked how the frogs' eggs were doing.

"By the time we get to school tomorrow, I think that most of them will have eaten their way right out of the jelly," said Mandy. "It won't be long now before the pond is full of tadpoles!"

The next day, Mandy and James hurried to look at the frog spawn before school started. Mandy managed to reach the pond just ahead of James. "Yes!" she shouted. "Today *is* hatching day!"

"Gosh, there must be hundreds of them, just in this part of the pond alone!" said James, staring down at the newly hatched tadpoles clinging to the water plants and the rest of the spawn.

Some of their classmates saw them by the pond and hurried over to join them.

"I think they've *all* hatched," said Mandy, running around the pond to check.

"They haven't got mouths," said Lisa Glover, peering at the tadpoles clinging to the leaves of a water violet. "So how do they get food?"

"I think they sort of suck it in through their bodies," said James.

"So when do they get mouths?" asked Jill Redfern.

"I can't remember," said Mandy. "We'll have to wait and see."

It only took two days for the tadpoles' mouths to develop. "You can see their eyes properly now, too," Mandy said to James. "And the little gills on the outside of their chest that they breathe through."

"Isn't it funny how each separate group stays close together?" James pointed out.

"They'll soon split up from their own nurseries and swim around the pond," said Mandy. "Just wait and see."

As the weeks went by, the tadpoles' bodies became thicker and shorter and their back legs started growing. But Libby still wasn't interested, and Mandy felt more and more worried about her. The little girl was so quiet. Mandy even heard Susan Davis tell Nikki Simpson, another one of Libby's classmates, that she was really fed up with Libby. "I didn't see her at all during vacation. She didn't want to come over to my house, and she didn't ask me to go up to the farm, either."

Nikki nodded. "And whenever we have our lessons outside in the garden, she just sits there. It's like she doesn't care," she said.

One day, their class teacher, Miss Oswald, brought out a jar and a big plastic bowl. She passed the jar to Mandy and told her to dip it in the pond to try and catch some tadpoles. The first time, Mandy only got water. "Pour the water into the bowl and try again." Miss Oswald laughed.

This time, Mandy managed to get some tadpoles as well. Everyone crouched over the bowl so they could get a closer look.

"They've got toes!" Susan said excitedly.

"Where?" asked Nikki, joining in the crowd around Mandy. "Oh, I see. On their back legs."

"Do you remember how funny and stumpy their back legs looked when they first started growing?" Susan giggled. "That was two weeks ago. And, today, the tadpoles are just over seven weeks old. I counted it on the wall chart in the classroom."

Mandy sighed. She wished Libby was having as much fun as her friends. But Libby was standing outside the group — not at all interested in how the tadpoles had grown.

"The tadpoles' front legs are growing, too, aren't they, Miss Oswald?" asked Peter Foster.

"That's right, Peter, but the little plates covering the tadpoles' gills are hiding them," the teacher replied. "At this stage, the tadpoles breathe through the gills, but once their lungs have developed, the gills will disappear and we'll be able to see the front legs as well."

"Oh, I can't wait to see them with four legs," said Laura Baker. "I hope the gills don't disappear over the weekend when we aren't here."

"That stage is two *weeks* away, not two days!" laughed Miss Oswald. "But now," she added, "before I empty the bowl back into the pond, I'm going to let you take turns dipping your hands in and see if you can get some tadpoles to wriggle over them. Keep your hands under the water, though, so the tadpoles won't feel frightened."

All Libby's friends squealed and giggled when their turn came to dip their hands into the bowl. But nobody could persuade Libby to join in the fun. "I'm going to look for butterflies," she said. And she walked away.

Mandy couldn't bear to see Libby looking so lonely. "Libby's a little worried about Heather, one of the new hens," she said quietly to the others. "My mom's been up to the farm to see her a couple of times this week. Poor Heather's got sore spots on her chest and she isn't eating properly."

"So that's what's wrong with Libby!" said Susan. "I'll make a get-well card for Heather. Maybe that will help."

"That's a nice idea," said Mandy. She knew Heather wasn't the only reason Libby was acting the way she was. But a card from Susan might help Libby to feel a bit better.

*   *   *

The next day, James and Mandy went up to Blackheath Farm with Mandy's grandma. They were taking Mrs. Masters a baby outfit Grandma had knitted. "I've also made a sweater for Libby," said Grandma, "so she won't feel left out." Mandy had told her grandmother that Libby wasn't very happy about the idea of a new baby.

When they arrived at the farmhouse, Mrs. Masters said Libby was somewhere outside so Mandy and James left Grandma and Mrs. Masters to have a chat and went to look for her. On their way, they stopped to watch the hens scrabbling and running around.

"They look like those wind-up toys," said James. "You know, you wind them up and they jerk across the floor with their heads bobbing up and down."

Mandy laughed and called to Rhonda. The red hen started to scuttle toward them. "There's another one coming, as well!" said Mandy. "I think it's Heather."

As Heather drew level with Rhonda, the

Rhode Island Red clucked noisily. Then, suddenly, she turned her head and started pecking Heather's chest.

"That must hurt her!" said James in amazement. "Rhonda has always seemed so gentle in the past."

Just then, Libby came out of one of the hen houses and called to her friends. At the sound of Libby's voice, Rhonda turned and Heather scuttled away.

"Libby! We just saw Rhonda pecking at Heather — it was awful!" Mandy explained quickly.

"Oh, Rhonda!" Libby cried. "So that's what's been upsetting Heather." She looked down at the ground, kicking the dust up with her shoe and then murmured, "We'd better go and tell Mom about it. I hope she won't be cross with Rhonda."

"Maybe Rhonda's feeling jealous of the extra attention you've been giving Heather," Mrs. Masters told Libby when she heard about Rhonda pecking Heather.

"Oh, poor Rhonda!" gasped Libby, dashing toward the door. "I'd better go and have a talk with her."

Mandy and James stayed with Grandma and Mrs. Masters. This was something Libby had to do on her own.

A little later, Libby came back in with Rhonda in her arms. "I've told her I love her as much as ever and she has no need to be jealous," she said. "But I feel really sorry for her," she added, stroking Rhonda's red feathers.

"I feel sorry for both the hens," said James. "Rhonda's miserable because she's jealous, and Heather's probably miserable, too, because Rhonda won't be friends with her."

"Rhonda probably feels a bit like you feel about having a baby brother or sister, Libby," Mandy said quietly.

"Yes," said James. "But, like you've told her, giving Heather some attention doesn't change the way you feel about *Rhonda,* does it, Libby?"

Soon after that, Grandma said it was time to go. For once, Libby didn't suggest that she and Rhonda walk to the gate with them. She was still nursing the hen and she looked very thoughtful.

6

"Raining Frogs!"

On Monday morning, when Mandy looked out of her bedroom window, she saw that it had been raining hard. The trees were dripping and there were puddles everywhere.

When Mandy met up with James, her friend couldn't wait to get to school. "It'll be the first time our class will be able to measure the rainfall," he said as they hurried along.

They reached school just as Mr. Masters was dropping off Libby. Libby called out to Mandy, so she stopped and waited for her. James went on ahead to check his class's weather project. Libby was wearing the new sweater Mandy's grandmother had knitted her.

"Hello, Libby," Mandy said. "That sweater really suits you."

"Oh, I love it. And I think the baby will love the outfit your grandma knitted, too. I've written her a thank-you note."

"That's nice, Libby. Grandma will be pleased you like them," Mandy said, feeling happy because Libby had actually mentioned the baby.

Libby smiled. "See you later," she said as she ran off to join a few of her classmates.

Mandy wondered what had happened to make Libby feel better about things. At morning break, she noticed Libby yelling and laughing with her friends. It was great to see her more like her usual self again.

During lunch, Mandy and James went to look in the wild patch to see if there were any frogs. Mandy saw Libby and Susan Davis by the pond, so she went over to talk to them. "You seem cheerful today, Libby," she said.

Libby smiled. "I've decided to be friends with the new baby when it comes," she said. "Then we won't be miserable like Rhonda and

Heather. But," she added, "hopefully if I spend lots of time with both of them together *they'll* make friends, too."

Mandy smiled. She was glad Libby was going to be friends with her brother or sister.

"So," said James after they'd left the two younger girls, "it looks like Libby's problems are over."

Mandy nodded. "But I bet she can't wait for the new baby to arrive now, and it's not due for weeks yet!"

For the next couple of weeks, Mandy didn't see much of Libby: It rained almost every day and there were no sessions in the school garden.

Then, late one Sunday afternoon, Mr. Masters made an anxious phone call to Animal Ark. "The baby's decided to arrive early," he said. "Could Libby possibly stay with you until her grandmother arrives? It might take her a while to get here — she's got to come by train and bus, and they're not very regular on Sundays."

"No problem. I'll come and pick up Libby

right away," said Dr. Emily. "How about letting her stay overnight? Then she can go to school with Mandy in the morning. That will save you worrying about how she'll get there."

Mandy was thrilled at the idea of Libby sleeping over. "I'll take the camp bed into my room and make it up while you're getting her, Mom," she suggested.

When Libby arrived, Mandy took her up to her bedroom to show her where she'd be sleeping. "I'll be able to tell all my friends I slept at Animal Ark while Mom went into the hospital to have the baby," Libby said excitedly. "I'll tell them I had animals sleeping in my bed, too!" she giggled, pointing to the furry toys Mandy had put on the pillow.

"They're called Nicholas, Toby, and William," said Mandy as the two girls made their way downstairs.

Dr. Emily was just putting the phone down when they went into the kitchen. "That was Grandpa," she said. "He's just seen Croaker sitting in her patch, and she seems to be in excellent condition. He wondered if you'd like to go around and see her."

"Oh, yes, please," said Mandy. There was a knock on the back door. "Here's James and Blackie. Let's go to Lilac Cottage right away, before it starts raining again."

But it started raining heavily when they were almost at the village square. "Run for the big oak tree!" said James. "It isn't stormy, so it'll be safe under there."

Suddenly Libby gasped and pulled hard at Mandy's arm. "Look!" she squealed. "It's raining frogs. There are loads and loads of them!"

There were big frogs, medium-sized frogs, dark-green and light-green frogs, all leaping around. Some of them were jumping really high — and it really did look as if they were falling from the sky with the huge raindrops.

"Make Blackie stand still, James," Libby said. "Otherwise he might squish one!"

"You're right, they're everywhere!" said James. "Sit, Blackie. Sit!" he said, pushing on the dog's back.

But Blackie didn't want to sit. The frogs looked like they were having fun and he wanted to join in the game. He tugged really hard at his leash — almost pulling James over — and Libby squealed again. "He nearly stepped on one. I'm sure he did. Do something, Mandy, quick!"

Watching her step, and laughing at James's efforts to control Blackie, Mandy crouched down in front of the puppy. Blackie barked excitedly and jumped on to Mandy's knees. Mandy ended up flat on her back, with Blackie on top of her.

When the three friends had stopped laughing, they looked around for the frogs. But they all seemed to have disappeared. "Well, at least it gave the frogs time to get away safely to wherever they're going!" said James as he pulled Blackie off Mandy.

"And we're all soaked now. We may as well forget about shelter and go straight to Grandma and Grandpa's," said Mandy. "We can't get any wetter!"

"Good heavens!" said Grandma when they arrived. "You look like drowned rats. Get your wet things off quickly while I get some towels."

While Mandy, James, and Libby rubbed themselves dry, Grandma dried Blackie off.

"I think you'll have to see Croaker another time," said Grandpa, coming into the kitchen. "It doesn't look as if it's going to stop raining for hours!"

"Never mind. It's just good to know Croaker's okay. And we saw lots of other frogs today," Mandy said, looking at her friends and laughing. In a fit of giggles they told Grandma and Grandpa all about the frogs in the square.

"I wish I could have seen it raining frogs!" Grandpa chuckled. "But next time I think I'd leave Blackie at home," he added, eyeing Mandy's muddy clothes and grinning.

7

Exciting News

Early next morning, Dr. Emily hurried into Mandy's bedroom. Libby was sitting on her bed while Mandy read her a story. Dr. Emily smiled and handed Libby the cordless phone. "It's your dad," she said.

"Dad! Has Mom had the baby?" Libby asked excitedly.

Mandy moved her head closer to Libby's and heard Mr. Masters say that Libby had a baby brother. "He's got dark, curly hair like yours, Libby," he said. "His face is pink and a bit wrinkled, and Mom says to tell you that when he cries he sounds like a kitten meowing!"

Libby giggled, then her dad continued. "Mom and I thought you might like to pick a name for him."

"Boys' names . . ." Libby said thoughtfully. "I know!" She looked across at Mandy's furry toys. "I like Nicholas, Toby, and William."

Mandy and Dr. Emily glanced at each other and tried not to laugh. Mandy was glad none of her stuffed animals was called Snuggles!

Then Mandy wriggled out of bed to leave Libby to chat with her dad. "I want to write out an announcement to pin up on the school bulletin board," she whispered to her mom. The bulletin board was on the wall in the school hall. It was a great way of spreading news quickly.

Libby was delighted when she came down to

breakfast and saw the announcement Mandy had written out:

CONGRATULATIONS TO THE MASTERS FAMILY. LIBBY HAS A BABY BROTHER!

"I didn't know which name you'd decided on," Mandy told Libby. "I thought you could write that part yourself."

Libby smiled. She said she'd decided to wait until she'd seen her baby brother before making up her mind. Then she asked if they could eat their breakfast quickly and get to school early. "I want some time to tell my friends everything that's happened!"

Mandy thought she'd better call James. "Otherwise he might stand waiting for us when we've already left," she explained.

The sky was blue and the sun was shining and there were quite a few people out and about when Mandy and Libby walked down the main street. Libby stopped to tell everyone they met that she had a baby brother, so James caught up with them halfway to school.

In the end, the three of them arrived just as the bell rang! "I'll ask Mrs. Todd if I can go and put the announcement on the bulletin board before assembly," Mandy told Libby as they hurried off to join their own classes.

By the time morning break came, everyone knew about Libby's baby brother. And, after break, Mandy and some of the other helpers went to join the younger children in the school garden. Their report was almost finished: This was going to be their last session.

Libby was still so excited that Mandy wondered if the little girl would be able to concentrate. But when they reached the pond, they found that most of the tadpoles were now baby froglets — their tails had almost disappeared and they could breathe out of the water.

As Mandy and Libby stood there, the tiny frogs kept popping out of the water to sit on stones and lily pads. "That one's darker than the others," said Mandy, pointing. "It's the

same color as the last frog we rescued from Farmer Jessop's cattle grid. James and I called it Legs — I bet that dark froglet is one of Legs's babies!"

Suddenly, Libby grabbed Mandy's arm. "Look, Mandy!" she said urgently. "One froglet has jumped right out of the pond!"

Mandy nodded. For a couple of minutes she and Libby watched in silence as the tiny frog hopped and jumped around the edge of the pond. But suddenly it turned and made its way toward the wild patch.

"We'd better follow it," Mandy whispered. "I'll see if I can pick it up and bring it closer to the pond. I'm sure it isn't big enough to live away from the water yet."

The wild patch was a mass of bluebells, cowslips, buttercups, daisies, and red clover, and the cuttings Grandpa had planted had grown bigger. At first, Mandy and Libby couldn't see the little frog.

Then a movement caught Mandy's eye and she pointed to a clump of plants.

Libby's eyes widened as she saw two frogs sitting under the leaves — the baby frog and a much bigger one. "I think the larger frog is the froglet's older sister, waiting for the baby to grow big enough so they can play together!" she said. "Just like *I'll* be waiting for my baby brother to grow up!"

"I suppose the big sister will show the baby the way back to the pond," said Mandy. "Come on, Libby. Let's go and write down what we've seen today. It makes a fantastic end to your report."

"It does," Libby agreed. "But I hope our baby froglets will stay here and live in the wild patch."

"Because they hatched in our pond, they might return to it when it's time for them to lay their own frogs' eggs," said Mandy. "You'll be about eight or nine by then, Libby. Perhaps you'll get to help younger children learn all about the life cycle of frogs, like I have with you!"

"Maybe my brother will be at school by

then," said Libby. "I could be *his* helper. Oh, Mandy, I can't wait to see him!"

When Mandy arrived at Animal Ark after school, Bill Ward was in the waiting room with Tara. Mandy hurried over to say hello. "You're getting to be such a big girl," said Mandy, laughing as the puppy licked her neck. "Is Tara here for her second vaccination, Mr. Ward?"

Bill Ward nodded. "How would you like to take her into the treatment room, Mandy? Your dad says it will be okay."

Mandy felt so proud as she carried the puppy into the treatment room. She held Tara carefully on the treatment table and watched as Dr. Adam ran gentle hands all over the puppy's body. Then he listened to Tara's heart before checking her eyes, ears, and the inside of her mouth.

"Everything's fine," Dr. Adam said, stroking Tara's head. "Now for the nasty part. Ready, Mandy?"

Mandy nodded and held Tara still. She told the puppy that she'd just feel a tiny jab and that it was nothing to worry about. "It's to stop you from getting sick. Very soon, Mr. Ward will be able to take you for walks in the park. And down by the river and in the square," she added.

Tara looked up at Mandy as if she under-stood every word. She didn't even notice Dr. Adam injecting her.

"Right, that's it," Dr. Adam said. "You can take her home now, Mandy."

"Take her home?" Mandy repeated.

Dr. Adam looked at Mandy's puzzled face and smiled his lopsided grin. "Mr. Ward and I arranged it," he said. "We thought you'd like to see how well Tara and Delilah have settled down together. He's gone on ahead to tell Mrs. Ward and Delilah that they're having com-pany."

It wasn't far to the Wards', but Mandy's arms were aching by the time she reached their house on the main street. Mrs. Ward opened the front door with Delilah in her arms. "Delilah's been looking everywhere for Tara since Bill came back alone," she said as Mandy thankfully put Tara down on the hall floor.

Mrs. Ward put Delilah down as well. For a moment, puppy and kitten just stood still looking at each other. Then Delilah put out a paw and banged Tara gently on the nose. Tara lifted one of her paws and, just as gently, banged the side of the kitten's head. The next minute the two of them bounded up the stairs, then all the way down again.

Mandy and Mrs. Ward laughed loudly, and Bill appeared out of the front room to see what was going on. The three of them watched as, side by side, the animals made their way into the kitchen, Delilah with her tail held high and Tara wagging hers in crazy circles.

When Mandy, prompted by Bill, crept after them, she saw them clamber into Tara's basket to lie down together. "They're turning out to be very good friends," Mr. Ward whispered from behind Mandy. "I'll have to get a kitty leash. I've got a feeling, when I start taking Tara for walks, that Delilah will want to come, too."

Later, back at Animal Ark, Mandy told her parents everything that had happened when she'd taken the puppy home. "It was great that he let me take Tara into the treatment room for her vaccination. I can't wait until I'm old enough to help out properly with the animals."

"I think your middle names should be 'Can't Wait,' Mandy!" Dr. Emily laughed.

"So should Libby's," Mandy said. "She can't wait to see her baby brother. She won't have long to wait now, though."

The next day, while Mandy and James were having a quick look at the frogs in the school pond before school started, Libby came running over. "I've seen him!" she said. "I've seen my brother. Dad took me to the hospital last night. He's gorgeous, Mandy. Mom's bringing him home today. And I didn't choose Toby, Nicholas, *or* William!"

"So what name *did* you choose?" Mandy asked, laughing at Libby's excitement.

"Ryan," said Libby. "It really suits him, Mandy. Mom said he sounded like a cat meowing when he cries, but I think it sounds like he's saying 'Ryan, Ryan, Ryan.' And Ryan Masters sounds good, doesn't it?"

"It sounds great," said Mandy. "I can't wait to see him myself."

"Mom says you and James can be his first visitors when we bring him home," said Libby.

Then she ran off to tell her classmates all about her little brother.

"A lot's happened since we came back to school after Easter, hasn't it, James?" Mandy said. "We had the frog rescue, bringing the frog spawn here and watching the tadpoles turn into frogs. Libby's got a baby brother, Rhonda's friends with Heather, Delilah's friends with Tara, and everything in the new school garden

is growing well." Mandy looked fondly at the tiny froglets leaping from one lily pad to another. "And," she added, "we've made new frog friends. I wonder what will happen next?"

"I don't think there's anything left to happen," James replied.

Mandy didn't agree. "There's *always* something happening in Welford," she laughed.